A Little Problem

Written by Karen Tayleur
Illustrated by Melissa Webb

sundance™

Published by
Sundance Publishing, LLC
33 Boston Post Road West
Suite 440
Marlborough, MA 01752
1-800-343-8204
www.sundancepub.com

Copyright © text Karen Tayleur
Copyright © illustrations Melissa Webb

First published 2002 by
Pearson Education Australia Pty. Limited
95 Coventry Street
South Melbourne 3205 Australia
Exclusive United States Distribution: Sundance Publishing

Guided Reading Level J
Guided reading levels assigned by Sundance Publishing using the text characteristics
described by Fountas & Pinnell in their book *Guided Reading,* published by Heinemann.

ISBN 978-0-7608-5804-2

Printed by Nordica International Ltd.
Manufactured in Guangzhou, China
April, 2010
Nordica Job#: 04-23-10
Sundance/Newbridge PO#: 225906

Contents

Characters

Helen Little is very tall. She dreams of being a gymnast but thinks she is too tall.

Joseph Rickman is also very tall. He would much rather play the saxophone than basketball.

Ron Blair is short. He wants to be tall like Joseph.

Chapter One

The Little Household

Helen Little was definitely not little like her name. In fact, Helen Little was very tall for her age. This caused quite a few problems in her life.

"One child's ticket," she'd say at the train station.

"Are you sure?" the ticket person would ask.

Helen hated to make a fuss. Sometimes she would just pay the extra money for an adult ticket.

She hated people looking at her as if there was something wrong with her.

"My goodness," many people would say. "Aren't you a tall one?"

"How original," Helen would mutter under her breath. She wished people would just leave her alone.

Her relatives would ask her to stand
back-to-back with her cousins.

"Do you think Sam has grown,
George?"

"Of course, Maria. Can't you see? He's
nearly past Helen's elbow now."

Helen hated being used as a ruler.

Helen tried everything she could think of to stop herself from growing taller. She watched TV with a brick on her head. She ate shortbread cookies. She wore baggy clothes to make her body look smaller. But no matter what she did, she always stood out above the crowd.

But there was one place where Helen felt comfortable. That was in the Little home with her family.

Dad Little was a very tall man. He had to stoop to go through most doorways.

Mom Little wasn't much shorter. She didn't bother with high heels.

"Uncomfortable things," she'd complain. "I don't need them anyway."

Rags Little was the scruffiest, bounciest, smelliest dog you would ever meet. He was part poodle. Helen always wondered which part that was. Rags was the size of a Shetland pony.

In the Little home, Helen almost felt short. Unfortunately, she couldn't always stay at home.

Chapter Two

The Oak Street Gym

Across the road from Helen's upstairs bedroom window was the Oak Street Gymnastics Club. Helen knew this because it said so in large, orange letters on the old, gray building. People walked in and out of the building all day, Monday through Saturday.

Helen saw little girls wearing pink tights and boys with sweaty heads coming out of the gym. Older girls with strange hair styles talked so loudly that their voices floated up to Helen's window.

Helen didn't know exactly what went on in the Oak Street Gym. But she was very curious to find out.

One night Helen watched the Olympic gymnasts on television. They looked very graceful on the balance beam. She tried to balance along the end of her bed. Arms out to the side. One foot in front of the other. Rags watched, wagging his tail. She wibbled. She wobbled. Her foot caught in her large, floppy pants. She fell.

"Helen?" Her mother popped her head into Helen's bedroom. "What are you doing?"

Helen was on the floor. She grabbed a book and looked up at her mother. "I just dropped this book I was reading for school," she said.

At school there were many sports, but
no gymnastics. In class, Helen sat at the
back so the other kids could see the board.
She was surprised one day to find someone
else's books in the back row beside her.
At the front of the room, Mrs. Mullens,
the teacher, clapped her hands loudly.

"Quiet, everyone. Please meet your new classmate, Joseph Rickman. He's just moved here, so let's make him feel welcome."

Joseph was sitting in the chair next to Mrs. Mullens. He stood up. And up. And up. He was as tall as the teacher!

Helen gasped. Someone gave a low whistle. Someone else laughed.

"That's enough, class. You may go back to your seat now, Joseph," said Mrs. Mullens.

Joseph made his way to the back of the room and sat next to Helen.

My goodness, thought Helen. Here's someone who is actually taller than I am.

Joseph looked at her, and Helen shrank into her large clothes.

Chapter Three

The Basketball Court

That day at lunch Helen sat under a tree near the basketball court. She watched Joseph over the top of her book.

Some boys were playing basketball nearby and asked Joseph to join them.

"No, thanks," he said.

"Come on," said one boy.

"Don't be a wimp," said another.

"I don't play basketball," said Joseph.

The crowd of boys laughed.

"No. Really. I don't even know the rules," Joseph tried again.

A short boy pushed his way to the front of the group. He spun a basketball on one finger. The name RON was scratched in big letters on the ball.

"What's to know, Stretch?" he asked.

"My name's Joseph."

The boy threw the ball at Joseph and hit him on the chest. The ball popped back and hit Ron in the head.

Everyone laughed. Even Helen giggled into her book.

"You're supposed to catch the ball, Stretch." Ron's ears were red.

Joseph stood still, his arms loose at his sides.

"Leave him alone, Ron," said someone in the group.

"I know," said Ron, smiling at Joseph. "You stand at the end of the court. Make your arms into a circle, and we'll use you for the hoop."

"Let's go, guys," said one of the boys.

The crowd moved away.

"We'll play later," said Ron, looking at Joseph.

Turning away, Ron saw Helen watching him.

"Hey, Little," he yelled at Helen. "You could stand at the other end of the court. A pair of basketball hoops."

He laughed again and ran off.

Helen walked over to Joseph.

"That's Ron," Helen explained.

"Uh-huh."

"He's a real pain. He's always showing off. No one likes him."

Joseph just shrugged.

"Happens all the time," he said.

"What do you like to do?" asked Helen.

"I play saxophone," said Joseph.

"You're really tall," Helen blurted out. She couldn't believe she'd said that. She hunched down into her clothes.

Joseph walked away. "You're not so short yourself," he said quietly.

Chapter Four

Folk Dancing Class

That afternoon was folk dancing class. The following Saturday evening there was going to be a dance to show what the kids had learned.

"You don't have to come," Helen told her parents. Helen hated folk dancing.

Some girls wore skirts that swirled around and around. They never looked down at their feet. They never tripped up their dance partner. Well, hardly ever.

"Now, twirl your partners," said Mrs. Mullens, tapping her feet.

Helen wondered where Joseph was. She was sorry she'd said he was really tall.

Looking around for Joseph, Helen accidentally lifted up her dance partner.

"Put me down, Little," Ron hissed. His feet were in the air.

"Oh," she said and dropped him.

The music stopped, and Mrs. Mullens clapped her hands. Then she talked to them about the upcoming dance.

Helen looked around the room. Ron stuck out his tongue at her. She shrank back into her clothes.

". . . skirts," the teacher was saying. "Just any old skirt you have at home will do . . ."

Oh great, thought Helen. I don't have any old skirts at home. I don't even own a skirt or a dress.

". . . lovely food, and a real band playing for us."

I just won't go, thought Helen.

On Saturday morning, Mom Little took Helen shopping for a skirt.

"I don't have to go," said Helen. "It's just a dumb old dance."

"Of course you're going," said her mother.

Mom Little pressed the Women's Department button in the elevator.

Helen hated shopping for clothes. Nothing in the kids' section fit her. And the clothes in the women's section were too old for her. Mom Little rushed out of the elevator ahead of her.

Helen dragged her feet, not looking where she was going.

She bumped into someone.

"Sorry," she said. Then she looked up into the frowning face of Joseph.

Chapter Five

Feeling Tall

"What . . . what are you doing here?" Helen asked.

"I'm with my mom," Joseph said. He pointed toward the makeup area.

"Oh, I thought you might have been buying a skirt," Helen said, trying to joke with Joseph.

"I'm not dancing," said Joseph, still frowning.

"Lucky you," said Helen. "Is Ron giving you a hard time?"

Joseph shrugged.

"Ron just feels bad because he's short for his age," said Helen. She didn't know how she knew this. But suddenly it made sense.

Helen pictured Ron playing basketball. He was a good player, but he had trouble with some shots because of his height.

"I've always wanted to be shorter," said Joseph.

"You, too?" asked Helen.

Joseph nodded.

"People," said Helen, "the things they say . . ."

"Have you been stretching yourself?" quoted Joseph.

"Are you sure you're only ten?" said Helen, laughing.

"How's the weather up there?" said Joseph, smiling.

"Legs right up to your armpits," said Helen.

They both laughed.

"I've always wanted to be a gymnast," said Helen suddenly.

"Why don't you try?" asked Joseph.

"Gymnasts are small," she said.

"Who said?"

Helen thought of the Oak Street Gym across from her bedroom window. The kids going in and out of the building had always seemed so much shorter. She told Joseph about it.

"Of course, they seem shorter," he said. "Looking down from your window, everything looks smaller."

Helen nodded slowly. She stood up straighter.

"I wish you were going to the dance tonight. . . . Hey!" she said. "Do you really play the saxophone?"

"Why?" asked Joseph.

"I've just had a great idea."

That night Helen danced with Ron. She was careful. She didn't look at her feet. Mom Little had made her a new skirt that swirled around and around.

"Not bad, Little," said Ron as the music stopped.

"You're a good dancer," said Helen.

Ron's ears turned pink. He grinned
and said, "Yeah. Well . . ."

Helen looked over Ron's head and
waved to Joseph. He was standing on the
stage with the band. A group of kids were
gathered around him.

"Stretch can really play that
saxophone," said Ron.

"His name's Joseph," said Helen, looking back over at Joseph with a smile on her face. Because of him, she was now the newest member of the Oak Street Gymnastics Club.